First Edition

OPEN SEASON™

Best Buddies

Written by
Julia Simon-Kerr

HarperKidsEntertainment
An Imprint of HarperCollins Publishers

The town of Timberline was Boog's home
and his favorite place in the whole world.
He lived in the warm, cozy garage of a local forest ranger.

But Boog wasn't at home in his warm bed.
He was lost in the forest during hunting season!
Boog's new friend Elliot was leading them out of the forest and back home.
There was just one problem—
Boog was starting to think Elliot didn't know the way home.

When they passed the very same beaver dam
that they had seen the day before,
Boog knew he was right.
Elliot was leading them in circles!

Just when Boog was telling Elliot exactly
what he thought of him—KABLAM! A blast broke
the silence of the forest. It was the hunters!

While all of the wild animals took cover,
Boog did the only thing he could think of—he ran!

KA-CRACK! Boog looked down and realized
he had run onto a beaver dam . . . and the dam was breaking!

Boog was swept down the river with Elliot
and the other animals close behind him!

But Boog had had enough! He just wanted to get back to Timberline, and he wasn't going to get there if he kept following Elliot.

Boog made a decision.
He took off for Timberline by himself, just as it started to rain.

When he found a cabin in the middle of the forest,
Boog couldn't wait to get out of the cold. *Civilization!* he thought.

But when Boog turned on the cabin light,
he realized he'd made a terrible mistake.

This was Shaw's hunting cabin!
Boog needed to get out of there, and fast.

Boog bolted from the cabin before Shaw caught him.
But he couldn't stop thinking about the other animals.

As he was running out, he noticed Shaw had mounted
Elliot's missing antler on the wall.
Boog was starting to think he shouldn't have left his friend behind.

Before Boog knew it, he tripped and fell right in the middle of a highway. He'd been so busy worrying about Elliot and the other animals that he hadn't looked where he was going. Then he noticed twinkling lights off in the distance. It was Timberline!

TIMBERLINE 5 mi

But Boog realized he couldn't go home just yet. He needed to find Elliot before the hunters did. They were a team. Elliot needed him, and he was starting to think he needed Elliot, too.

Boog headed back into the forest.
Elliot and the other animals were thrilled to see him.
Boog knew he and his buddy could do anything together.
They could even declare open season on the hunters!